Bantam Books in the Choose Your Own Adventure® Series
Ask your bookseller for the books you have missed

Choose Your Own Adventure® Series for young readers

UNDERGROUND KINGDOM

BY EDWARD PACKARD

ILLUSTRATED BY ANTHONY KRAMER

BANTAM BOOKS
TORONTO • NEW YORK • LONDON • SYDNEY • AUCKLAND

RL 4, IL age 10 and up

UNDERGROUND KINGDOM
A Bantam Book / March 1983

ISBN 0-553-23292-4

Published simultaneously in the United States and Canada

*Bantam Books are published by Bantam Books, Inc. Its trade-
mark, consisting of the words "Bantam Books" and the por-
trayal of a rooster, is Registered in U.S. Patent and Trademark
Office and in other countries. Marca Registrada, Bantam
Books, Inc., 666 Fifth Avenue, New York, New York 10103.*

PRINTED IN THE UNITED STATES OF AMERICA

O   0 9 8 7 6

For Caroline—
with appreciation and special
thanks for her counsel on
conflict resolution

WARNING!!!!

Do not read this book straight through from beginning to end! These pages contain many different adventures you can have as you try to reach the Underground Kingdom. From time to time as you read along, you will be asked to make a choice. Your choice may lead to success or to disaster! The adventures you have will be the result of the decisions you make. After you make your choice, follow the instructions to see what happens to you next.

SPECIAL WARNING!!!!

The Underground Kingdom is not easy to reach. Many readers never get there. Others never return.

Before starting out on your journey, you may want to read Professor Bruckner's theory, which is set forth on the pages that follow.

Professor Bruckner is a rather boring writer, and I wouldn't suggest that you bother to read his theory, except that, if you ever get to the Underground Kingdom, it might save your life.

Good luck!

PROFESSOR BRUCKNER'S THEORY

The discovery of the Bottomless Crevasse in Greenland by Dr. Nera Vivaldi supports my theory that the earth is not solid, as has been thought, but that it is hollow. The Bottomless Crevasse is probably the sole route from the earth's surface to a vast "Underground Kingdom." The only other possible link would be an underground river, flowing in alternating directions in response to the tides, but this seems unlikely.

How, you may ask, was the earth hollowed out? My studies show that more than a billion years ago a tiny black hole collided with our planet and lodged in its center, pulling the whole molten core into an incredibly massive sphere only a few hundred meters across.

If you were to stand on the inner surface of the earth, like a fly on the inner shell of an enormous pumpkin, you would see the black hole directly overhead, like a black sun.

The gravity of the earth's thick shell would hold you to the inner shell of the earth, though you would weigh much less than you would on the outer surface because the mass of the Black Sun would tend to pull you toward it. If there were a very tall mountain in the Underground Kingdom and you were to climb to the top of it, you might be pulled up into the Black Sun because gravity gets stronger as you approach a massive object.

In all other respects the Black Sun would not be dangerous to any creatures in the Underground Kingdom. On the contrary, the Black Sun would be necessary to life in the underworld, but in the opposite way that the sun is necessary to life on the earth's surface. Our sun gives us heat and keeps us from freezing. The Black Sun *absorbs* heat. If there *is* an underground kingdom, it is the Black Sun that keeps its inhabitants from being baked to death by the heat within the earth!

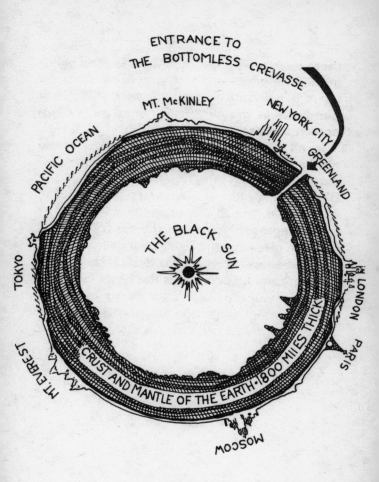

CHOOSE YOUR OWN ADVENTURE® • 18

UNDERGROUND KINGDOM

You are standing on the Toan Glacier in northern Greenland, staring down into the black void of the crevasse. You shiver as you wonder whether you were lucky or unlucky to be invited on this expedition.

Standing next to you are Gunnar Larsen of the National Research Institute and Dr. James Sneed, a geologist. A small black box containing a signal transmitter is suspended over the crevasse by two long poles. The transmitter is wired to a console a few yards away in the ice. Dr. Sneed turns a dial as he monitors the display screen.

"Well?" Larsen's voice is impatient.

Sneed looks up, a broad smile on his face. "This is it, friends—the Bottomless Crevasse."

"Any radar return?" Larsen asks.

Sneed shakes his head. "None."

For a minute no one speaks. Like you, the others must feel excited to have reached their goal but also a little sad. It was just a year ago that your old friend, Dr. Nera Vivaldi, radioed from this spot that she had reached the Bottomless Crevasse. A few moments later, her radio went dead. She was never seen again.

Go on to page 2.

Now you stand at the edge, lost in thought. How could the crevasse have no bottom? Could it really lead to an underground kingdom? What happened to Dr. Vivaldi?

But your thoughts are shattered. You didn't seem to slip, yet suddenly you are falling into the crevasse! A ledge is coming up fast beneath you. You could land on it, but you're falling so fast you're sure to be badly injured. You might only be saving yourself for a slow, agonizing death.

These thoughts race through your head in a split second.

*If you try to land on the ledge,
turn to page 5.*

If not, go on to the next page.

Your consciousness slips away as you fall faster down, down, down.

The next thing you know, you're floating in air. In the soft, reddish light you can see that you are in a cavern, drifting toward the ceiling—or is it the floor? In a flash you realize what has happened—*you've fallen to a point where gravity above you is almost equal to gravity beneath you!*

You brush against a firm surface—a wall that feels like clay. You cling to it for a moment. Then you're floating again, drifting slowly down. You begin to lose your fear as you realize that gravity here is so weak that you can fall mile after mile without being hurt. After a while you begin to relax and enjoy drifting through a fantastic twilight world. You only wish it weren't so hot! Closing your eyes, you try to pretend that you are safely home in bed.

Turn to page 6.

Your whole body is racked with pain as you crash onto the ledge. You're shaken and bruised but still alive! A snowbank cushioned your fall.

"HELP!" you cry.

"Hold on!" Larsen yells. "It's going to be tricky, but we're rigging our ropes. We'll get you up."

You feel a flash of joy; then you remember something that chills you to the bone. You were very careful not to fall in. You're quite sure you didn't slip; you were pulled as if by an unknown force within the Bottomless Crevasse.

Should you warn your friends about the strange force? If you do, they may be afraid to get close enough to rescue you.

If you warn Larsen and Sneed, turn to page 13.

If you just yell, "Please hurry!" turn to page 9.

Once again you brush against a firm surface. This time it's the floor of the cavern. In fact, you have touched down on the mossy bank of an underground stream. You drink from the cool, clear water, then step out of the cavern into this strange world.

The only illumination is a dim red-orange glow that seems to come from the ground. The air is so clear that you can see shadowy, curving hills and valleys stretching out in all directions, even above you.

Why do you feel so good? It must be because you are so light—you could hardly weigh more than ten or fifteen pounds. You spring to your feet. Every movement is easy. You jump—twenty or thirty feet high—and float gently to the ground.

Then you realize that you are not alone. Only a few yards away is an odd creature. As big as you are, it seems to be some kind of bird yet much more than a bird. Under a crown of soft golden feathers are enormous blue-green eyes, so vivid and intense that they seem to be not only a means of vision, but also a means of power.

There is something terrifying about that face, but also something angelic, something that draws you to it. In fact, you feel as if you are being hypnotized by those eyes—eyes of an angel bird!

If you run from the strange creature, turn to page 15.

If you hold your ground and face it, turn to page 10.

You run as fast as you can, hoping that once the mother sees her baby is safe, she will not pursue you.

You dart into a cavern. It's darker and hotter than the pleasant spot where you found the fledgling. Is it the same passageway you came through?

Still running, you look back over your shoulder to see if the mother bird is following. At that moment you find yourself falling, or rather rising, toward the earth's surface—drawn up into what must be the same shaft that forms the Bottomless Crevasse!

Soon you stop rising and start falling. Then you rise a shorter distance, stop, and begin to fall again. You feel like a yo-yo, bouncing up and down, up and down, until you finally come to rest at the center of gravity, the point where you will neither rise nor fall. Like a cork thrown in the ocean, you seem doomed to drift forever.

The End

"*Hurry!*" you yell.

A moment later you see Dr. Sneed's reassuring face on one side of the opening above you. Larsen peers over the other side. "Don't worry," he calls.

"*Hey, what's . . .*" Dr. Sneed's voice is cut off as he slides over the icy lip of the crevasse. You watch with horror as his body hurtles by, down into the abyss!

You yell at Larsen to get back from the edge. But a blur whirls by, and you feel the rush of air as his body plummets after Sneed's.

They're both gone, and now you are alone, trapped on a narrow icy ledge. If only you had warned them, you would have saved them and probably yourself too.

Now your chances look slim. A search helicopter might fly over. But will it land? Will anyone ever find you down here? Will you even survive the arctic night?

Turn to page 12.

You stand there and watch as the strange creature walks slowly toward you. Then you see the large, blue-white pieces of broken shell. This angel bird is only a fledgling, just hatched!

Losing your fear, you walk up and stroke the creature gently. It cocks its head to the side and touches you with one of its wings. At that moment it seems almost human.

But suddenly you hear a loud whirring sound. Hovering above you is another angel bird, a much larger one. It must be the mother of the fledgling. She swoops toward you.

If you run, turn to page 8.

If you grab the fledgling and try to use it to shield yourself, turn to page 14.

If you dive to the ground and shield your face with your arms, go on to page 11.

You dive to the ground and shield your face with your arms, hoping the angel bird will leave you unharmed.

Nothing happens; the angel bird must have taken her young one away. What's more, you begin to have the feeling that you are completely safe. Slowly you get to your feet. Standing nearby are three more of the large creatures. One of them effortlessly leaves the ground, glides through the air, and lands beside you. You have a strong urge to climb on its back.

Why is it you feel so safe? The angel birds begin to make musical sounds, more beautiful than anything you've ever heard. Is it this music that causes your good feelings, or something more? These creatures seem to communicate not in words, or even ideas, but in feelings.

Without thinking more about it, you leap up, and because there's very little gravity, you almost *float* onto the creature's feathery back. You nestle in. It feels like a bed of goose down, soft and silky.

Turn to page 16.

You look along the ledge. It curves up toward the surface, but it also becomes narrower. You try to gauge how close to the surface you could get without losing your footing. By cutting a couple of handholds in the ice with your pocket knife, you could make it to the top, if you don't lose your grip.

If you try to make it, turn to page 18.

If you decide to wait, turn to page 20.

"Get back from the edge!" you yell. *"I didn't fall, I was pulled in!"*

For a few moments you hear nothing; then Sneed yells, "Thanks for warning us. There may be some force here we don't understand. But don't worry, we're rigging a brace so we can pull you up without getting too close."

A few minutes later you see a nylon climbing rope dangling in front of you. You pull in enough to tie around your waist and under your arms. Taking a firm grip, you call up to the top, "I'm ready—pull away!"

Your heart skips a beat as you're yanked off the ledge. You dangle for a moment; then, slowly, foot by foot, your friends pull you up over the edge. You scramble across the ice into their arms.

"Thank goodness we got you!" says Larsen. "The Bottomless Crevasse is a killer. I think we'd better quit now."

"I agree. I've had enough," Sneed says.

After what you've been through, you're not about to argue with them. The three of you pack up and begin the long trek back across the glacier. You're happy to be alive, but you know that you'll always regret that you never reached the Underground Kingdom.

The End

You lunge for the baby bird, hoping that you can use it as a shield.

Even as you move, you feel a rush of wind as the mother dives to protect her baby. You realize that you've just made the stupidest decision of your life.

Strangely, the mother bird did not harm you. Instead, you feel that you have been put into a trance. Stranger still, you sense that *something has set time back*—that you are being given another chance!

Turn to page 10.

You run from the angel bird—up a hill that gets steeper and steeper. In the light gravity of the underworld you can run faster than a deer, even up this mountain. Twenty, thirty, forty feet at a bound! You feel even lighter than you did before. You try to leap only a few feet in the air, but you find yourself floating. There is no way you can get down. You are entombed between the ground above and the ground below.

You close your eyes. Then, instead of feeling warm, you feel cold; instead of feeling light, you feel heavy. Instead of floating, you're lying on a hard, cold surface. Opening your eyes, you see ice walls rising above you.

Now you understand. When you fell into the crevasse, you landed on this ledge, about thirty feet below the surface. You must have hit your head on the ice. What a strange dream you've had! It seemed so real—as if the angel bird put the dream in your head! But there are other things to think of right now.

"HELP!" you shout.

No one answers. Larsen and Sneed have probably given you up for lost.

Turn to page 12.

The angel bird glides through the canyons and corridors beneath the earth. It increases its speed, and you hold tight as it swoops through long, curving passageways. It's the most exciting ride of your life, and would certainly be the scariest if you didn't feel that you've never been safer.

Then, ahead of you, is a tunnel that flares out into a broad new world. An endless landscape stretches before you. It is bathed in soft, reddish light, as if the sun had just set everywhere around you!

A great river forms a curving line that divides the land. Trees line its banks. Farther back from the river are mountains, some of them lavender or blue and others that flicker like glowing embers. Strangely there is no horizon; instead the landscape fades into dusky reds and browns that curve over your head, forming a sky that is almost the same color as the ground. Directly above you is something that looks like the sun, but it is absolutely black!

So this is the Underground Kingdom—strange, vast, and very beautiful. What people or creatures live here? What mysteries does it hold? But you are swept from your daydreaming by the realization that your life here could be in danger.

If you set out to explore the Underground Kingdom, turn to page 19.

If you concentrate on getting safely back home, turn to page 22.

You inch your way along the edge, keeping your body flat against the wall of the crevasse. You should be able to make it, as long as you don't panic. You try not to look down.

After almost an hour of slow progress, you're able to raise a hand over the rim. But you still can't pull yourself up.

You hack away at the ice, gouging out another handhold, then another foothold. It seems like hours before you can take even one step higher. Then, with one great effort, you heave yourself over the edge, then twist and roll away from the deadly opening.

Stiff and shaky, you manage to stand and stare at the bleak world around you. The sun has set behind the western mountains, and you begin to shiver in the chill wind. You're thankful that in this part of Greenland it never grows dark in July. But it does grow cold—well below freezing—and you're too exhausted to run and jump to warm yourself.

Turn to page 21.

You know how you feel: the risks don't matter. You want to explore the Underground Kingdom!

The angel bird seems to understand. Steeply banking, it swoops down along the great river and glides gently onto a mossy plain. Nearby is a grove of tall trees. Short stumpy branches with clusters of multicolored leaves thrust out from their trunks. They look almost like hands holding bunches of flowers.

You slide to the ground, and at once the angel bird rises in the air. As it glides up into the dark red sky, you feel a wave of happiness. You follow its path with your eyes long after it has disappeared. Then, turning to survey the strange landscape, you wonder where you will go. What dangers await you?

Turn to page 40.

You decide not to risk the treacherous climb to the surface. Surely help is on the way. You huddle on the icy ledge, stamping your feet and clapping your hands, trying to keep warm. You feel your body temperature dropping. You've got to stay awake until a search party arrives.

The hours pass slowly. The sun dips below the horizon, but there is still light in the sky. Straining, you think you hear something. . . . *Pocka pocka pocka pocka pocka* . . . overhead. A chopper is hovering over the crevasse! For a moment you're blinded by a searchlight. The chopper drops to just a few yards above you. The crew lowers a harness. Eagerly you grab it and buckle it around you.

"HOLD ON. WE'RE PULLING YOU UP." Beautiful words over the bullhorn. You're suddenly yanked into the air. Moments later a pair of hands pulls you through the hatch. The pilot pours you a cup of hot chocolate from his Thermos.

"Thanks for staying alive till we got here," he says with a grin.

You soon feel life seeping back into your body. "Thanks for pulling me out!"

"This is the one place in the world everyone should stay away from," the pilot says.

"Nothing could get me back here," you say.

The End

There is no shelter from the relentless wind and no sign of Larsen or Sneed. It's getting hard to breathe. You soon begin to feel the dull aches, stiffness, and sick feeling you've read about—the dread symptoms of hypothermia; you are freezing to death. Maybe a search helicopter will arrive any moment. Maybe in a few hours. Maybe never.

You are very tired. You desperately need rest.

If you huddle in your parka and try to conserve your strength, turn to page 32.

If you force yourself to keep walking, turn to page 25.

Your strongest desire now is to be home again. You cling tightly to the angel bird. As if it knows what you're thinking, it rises in the air, banks steeply, and then, accelerating, hurtles into a corridor within the ground. You nestle into its thick downy coat as it streaks through the darkness. All the while you feel completely safe, and in time you sleep.

When you awake, it is much colder. A chill wind bites against your body. The brightness of the world around you is not the warm red light of the Underground Kingdom, but the cold white light of the Arctic. The barren landscape, pocketed with ice and snow, is a familiar scene, as is the rude village of shacks and tin-roofed buildings nearby. You're in Greenland! The village is the coastal settlement from which your party began its trek across the ice fields to the Bottomless Crevasse.

Go on to the next page.

As you trudge across the frozen slope to the village, you think about the angel bird and the Underground Kingdom, and you think how much more there must be in the universe, and even on our own planet, than we can ever imagine.

The End

"There's no chance of that," Professor Bruckner's assistant tells you. "An aerial photograph taken a few weeks ago showed that the glacier has moved, sealing the crevasse with 6,000 feet of solid ice."

You hang up the phone and stand by the window, thinking about the world that lies beneath the earth's surface. What is it like? What creatures might live there? What happened to Professor Bruckner? Did he find Larsen and Sneed? Is Dr. Vivaldi still alive? Now, of course, you'll never know.

The End

You force yourself to keep walking. If you wander too far from the crevasse, a search team might miss you, so you walk in a large square: fifty paces north . . . fifty east . . . fifty south . . . fifty west . . . fifty north . . . again . . . again. Your legs feel like lead. Your eyes are half shut. You hardly notice when the weak arctic sun reappears . . . the sun . . . you can't think . . . dizzy . . . you can't stand. . . .

It seems like another world when you wake up in a room with pale green walls and gleaming tile floors. Your head is swimming. What happened to Larsen and Sneed? You feel as if you've lived through a nightmare.

"You're lucky, we were able to save your leg." A tall, bearded doctor is speaking. "You'll be OK." Then his voice trails off as he tells you that your friends, Gunnar Larsen and Dr. Sneed, have joined Dr. Vivaldi, all lost forever.

"Larsen . . . Sneed." You keep mumbling their names until finally sleep comes.

By morning your head has cleared. It was a terrible ordeal, but at least you survived. In a few weeks you'll be home—home for good, because nothing could ever persuade you to go near the Bottomless Crevasse again!

Go on to page 26.

Three months have passed. You return home late one afternoon to find a man waiting at your front door.

"I'm Professor Bruckner. From the National Research Institute in Washington." He shakes your hand warmly.

"Please come in. Are you still studying the Bottomless Crevasse?"

Bruckner nods. "We've identified the force that may have pulled Larsen and Sneed into the crevasse. Would you be willing to go back? Precautions would be taken so there would be no chance of its happening again."

You shake your head. "I'm afraid not, Professor. I don't think I could go back to the place where my friends died."

Smiling, the professor leans toward you. "Would it change your mind if I told you that your friends may still be alive?"

"*What?*"

"It's true. We received faint radio signals from a point far beneath the earth's surface. I believe that one or more of the others must be alive somewhere in the Underground Kingdom, and we have the means to reach them. Now will you come?"

If you say that you'll go on the expedition, go on to page 28.

If you decide it would be too dangerous to go with Bruckner, turn to page 30.

"Professor Bruckner, count me in!"

"Good," he says. "This time we'll be far better equipped. NASA has put two helicopters at my disposal. One of them will transport our party of scientists and technicians. The other will carry the Vertacraft, a rocket-propelled capsule specifically designed for this mission."

Go on to the next page.

Three weeks later you find yourself staring once again at the Bottomless Crevasse.

"It looks narrower than when I was here before," you remark.

"Yes," Bruckner says, "the glacier has been advancing about three feet a year. It won't be long before the crevasse is completely sealed."

While you and the other members of the party stand at a safe distance, the professor cautiously walks to the rim of the crevasse. In one hand he holds an oblong instrument that emits an increasingly rapid clicking.

"Don't get too close!" you cry.

"Indeed." Bruckner takes a few steps back. "I think I know what happened to Larsen, Sneed, and Vivaldi."

"What?"

"Gravity waves coming from the center of the earth have disrupted space-time enough to pull them in." The professor looks down into your puzzled face. "And you, as well," he adds. "I've always suspected that the laws of physics may be different in the vicinity of a black hole. Now we have proof!"

"What does this mean?"

The professor smiles. "It means that the interior of the earth—beginning about 800 miles deep—is hollow."

Turn to page 75.

"No, thank you, Professor," you say. "I've seen enough. I never want to get near the Bottomless Crevasse again."

Bruckner shrugs. "I understand," he says as he holds out his hand.

From then on, you follow the news eagerly, hoping to hear some report on Professor Bruckner's expedition. One day, passing a newsstand, you see a headline that makes your heart sink: PROFESSOR AND PARTY MISSING IN WORLD'S MOST DANGEROUS ICE FIELDS!

In the months that follow you hear nothing further about the Bottomless Crevasse, until one night, watching the news, you hear an interview with two scientists who claim to have picked up radio signals coming from inside the earth. "We can't explain their seemingly impossible origin," one of them reports, "nor can we decipher the message, except for two words, *All Safe.*"

The next morning you call Professor Bruckner's office at the National Research Institute. "I was wondering whether there were any plans for another expedition to the Bottomless Crevasse," you say.

Turn to page 24.

You huddle in your parka, but the cruel wind penetrates your body. You feel yourself growing numb. You try to stand up, but your legs won't move. You feel as if you are drifting through time and space. Then you feel nothing at all.

The search and rescue team almost reached you in time. They were never able to locate Larsen and Sneed. A few days later a memorial service was held for the brave people who lost their lives exploring the Bottomless Crevasse. Everyone spoke very highly of you.

The End

"All right," says Bruckner, "if no one will volunteer, I'll go alone." The rest of you help position the Vertacraft over the crevasse and wish him well as he snaps the hatch shut and releases the craft into free-fall.

Hank Crouter, Bruckner's assistant, glances at his watch. "If he survives, we'll get a signal back within ten minutes," he says.

You all wait anxiously, watching the clock, watching the crevasse. Ten minutes go by, fifteen, twenty, twenty-five. A chilling wind bites through your parka. You kick the icy ground.

"Thirty minutes," says Crouter. "There's no way . . ."

Weary and sad, your party trudges back across the ice fields. The moving glacier is rapidly closing the crevasse. There won't be another chance.

The End

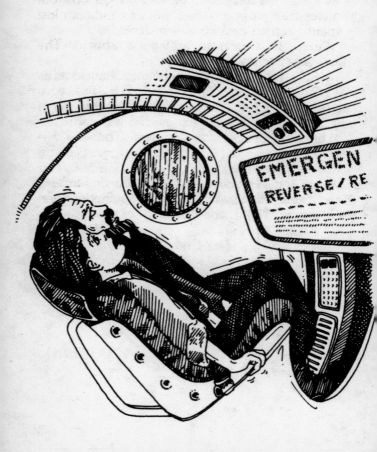

You know that your chances of surviving the expedition are slim. Even if you safely descend into the Bottomless Crevasse, there's no assurance that the Vertacraft will be able to get you out again. Still, it's your only chance to find your lost friends and to explore a new world.

You grit your teeth and climb aboard. The professor climbs in beside you.

"Ready?" he says. "I'm going to activate us as soon as we're centered."

"Ready." You strap yourself in and say a prayer. You feel like a larva inside a cocoon.

Looking through the port, you watch the others position the Vertacraft over the crevasse. You wave at them, and they wave back. *Suddenly you are falling—faster and faster, plummeting toward the center of the earth. Has the Vertacraft gone out of control?*

"Professor Bruckner!" you yell. "Won't the rockets work? Can't you slow us?"

"We're saving our fuel," he shouts. "Gravity will slow us—you'll see."

Has he gone mad? You notice a red button on the control panel. Next to it is a sign that reads:

EMERGENCY
REVERSE/RETURN TO INITIAL POSITION.

Turn to page 37.

You and Dr. Vivaldi cross the Great River and start your trek to the Shining Mountains. Along the way your guide, Mopur, brings back mountain game, breadbush, and tanga.

The air seems lighter and brighter than in the valley of the Great River. Never have you felt so happy as you do right now—hiking through the Shining Mountains.

But your Archpod guide grumbles and frets. He blinks and rubs his eyes.

Turn to page 92.

Thanks to the dual control system, it looks as if you have a chance to escape this madness. Still, you can't be sure it will save you. . . .

If you decide to push the Emergency-Reverse button, turn to page 89.

If you try to reason with Dr. Bruckner, turn to page 38.

38

"We're going too fast! Can't we slow down?" you call.

"No. We have hundreds of miles to go. We've got to get through the earth's mantle fast, or we'll be baked to death." Bruckner's voice is cool and reassuring. Maybe he knows what he's doing.

But every minute, the temperature rises. You begin to sweat. Whatever made you think you could survive such a trip? Sipping cold lemonade from a plastic bottle, you try to close your eyes and relax. Then it seems as if the Vertacraft is slowing, but you can't be sure.

Suddenly everything is still. The Vertacraft has come to rest. Looking through a porthole, you see that you have landed inside a large crater. Slowly you climb out of the Vertacraft and open the other compartment. Professor Bruckner's face is ashen gray. You feel for his pulse. Nothing. The strain of the descent must have been too much for his heart.

Turn to page 43.

You could probably climb a nearby tree and hide among the clusters of giant leaves. But is it wise to run like a frightened animal? Maybe things will go better for you if you bravely face the inhabitants of this world.

If you decide to face the creatures, turn to page 42.

If you decide to hide in a cluster-leaf tree, turn to page 46.

The scene around you reminds you of a photographic negative. All the shades and colors seem reversed. The ground is grayish pink clay with white outcroppings. In the distance you can see areas that glow like beds of hot coals. Nearby is a forest of trees with green trunks and white leaves. The trees are short; yet their branches, taking advantage of the light gravity, spread out for hundreds of feet in all directions.

You climb a small hill to get a better view. Wherever you look, the land curves upward, as if you were standing in the bottom of an enormous bowl. The sky is covered with what looks like reddish yellow clouds.

Most amazing of all is the sight directly overhead—a disc almost the size of the sun; but, instead of shining brightly, it is absolutely black. You can feel its coolness, as if it were drawing heat from your skin. It's the black hole at the center of the earth!

You turn sharply at the sound of chattering. Coming up the ravine are more than a dozen creatures, smaller than you, yet walking upright on two legs. Half human, half ape, they look like creatures that might have once lived on the earth's surface. They are carrying ropes and nets.

Turn to page 39.

You step forward to meet the strange procession. The underworld creatures form a circle around you, cackling and gesturing to each other.

You smile and hold out your arms. "Hello," you begin, but the creatures raise their nets and close in on you. One of them barks an order. They motion for you to follow them. You don't have much choice. Despite their small size, they move rapidly through the thick woods. Occasionally they freeze, and you hear them whispering, *"Kota, ib saben Kota."*

You march a mile or so through groves of trees. It's as hot as you've ever known it, and you feel as if you're going to faint, but finally you reach open land. Instantly you feel cooler. The Black Sun is drawing heat from your body.

Soon you reach a village of igloo-shaped structures that look as if they're made of green clay. One of your captors leads you to the nearest one. *"Ib agon,"* he says as he takes you inside.

Turn to page 44.

You bury the professor's body near the Vertacraft, and say a prayer. You feel sad and afraid of setting forth alone in a strange world. But there is no choice. You must search for food and shelter.

First, you've got to get out of this crater. There is a tunnel nearby. Peering inside, you see that it leads straight down. Suddenly you realize that it was through this tunnel that the Vertacraft traveled; you're looking through the other end of the Bottomless Crevasse. The tunnel doesn't lead straight down, but straight up—to the surface of the earth!

So Professor Bruckner was right. The earth is like a hollowed-out pumpkin, and you're standing on its inner shell. Your feet must be held to the ground by the gravity of the shell itself.

You look around at the walls of the crater. They are too steep to climb. But you feel so light—as if you were walking on the moon—you might be able to jump out.

You stand there a minute, wondering why the pull of gravity here isn't as strong as it is on the earth's surface. Then you remember the rest of Bruckner's theory: There is a black hole at the center of the earth, pulling you toward it. You leap as high as you can—twenty feet in the air! Then, with one great bound, you're out, standing on the surface of the Underground Kingdom.

Turn to page 40.

The interior of the agon, as it seems to be called, is lit by glowing stones circling the inner wall. In the center is a small fountain. Clear water bubbles forth and flows along a silver trough before disappearing underground. The floor is soft and spongy, like a thick bed of moss.

The leader steps forward. *"Ket,"* he says, pointing to himself. *"Ket Raka."* Pointing to the others, he says, *"Akim Raka, Tor Raka . . ."*

You repeat each name, then pointing to yourself, tell them your name. The Rakas laugh as they try to pronounce the strange sound.

Tor, who seems younger than the others, brings you something that looks like cheese but tastes like honey. Ket gives you a small pink fruit. *"Ib tanga,"* he says, smiling.

Tanga is delicious, and you are eating a second one when a large blue-furred Raka rushes into the agon. Pointing at you, he speaks excitedly in his own tongue. Tor begins to argue with him. The others join in.

"Nar mg calla!" the blue-furred Raka says loudly. It's clear he wants you to come with him; it seems likely that he represents the chief, or leader.

Ket and Akim gesture as if you should obey. But Tor shakes his head, warning you not to go.

If you follow the blue-furred Raka, turn to page 48.

If you refuse, turn to page 50.

You hide in the cluster-leaf tree. The strange creatures pass by except for one straggler, who stops to stretch. For a moment he looks right at you. *"Kota zaark!"* he cries, then turns and runs after the others.

Perhaps you needn't have been so cautious. The creature looked more like a frightened animal than a fierce hunter.

As you climb down from the tree, you hear a low moaning coming from the brush. A pair of bright blue lights is shining from within the darkness.

Go on to the next page.

Now the moaning comes from behind you. Turning, you see another pair of blue lights. Beneath them are long, glistening fangs. Slowly the creatures close in on you; their moans rise into high-pitched shrieks. What *are* they?

You have only a few seconds to live, so it hardly matters.

The End

Hoping for the best, you follow the blue-furred Raka to the center of the village. As you walk along the narrow footpaths, other Rakas emerge from their agons and stare at you curiously.

When you reach the central agon the blue-furred Raka lets out a long, low hooting noise, which is answered from within. Inside an old white-headed Raka sits near the central fountain. A large black disc hangs from his neck. For a long

time he stares at you. Finally he rises and steps closer. "So, you are what my hunters found. My name is Arton. I am the High Raka of the village of Rakmara."

You are so startled by the familiar words that it takes you a minute to answer. "How is it you speak my language?" you finally ask.

Arton smiles. "A visitor from the Nether World. She called herself Nera."

"Dr. Vivaldi? *She's alive? Where?*"

The old Raka shakes his head. "She tried to swim across the Great River. The river spirits have swallowed her."

"She might have made it across!" you say.

"Even if she did, the Archpods would have fed her to the Kota beasts."

"What are Archpods?"

"The Archpods live beyond the Great River. For a long time the Rakas and Archpods have each had one hunting boat; that is the law. Now the Archpods build many boats. They are not hunting boats; they are war boats. The Archpods plan to conquer Rakmara."

You hold your head in your hands. Poor Dr. Vivaldi! And now the threat of war.

Turn to page 51.

You shake your head and stand your ground. The blue-furred Raka glares at you and strides from the agon. He returns a few moments later with two other Rakas, each holding ropes and a net.

"I won't be taken captive like some animal!" you shout.

A Raka tries to rope you, but you duck out of reach. They draw closer. Like a football quarterback, you spin and dart past them.

"Kela! Zaark!" the Rakas yell, but you're already out of the agon, running across the dimly lit land.

Helped by the light gravity, you quickly reach a grove of cluster-leaf trees, and you keep running, on and on. At last you reach the open countryside. In the soft reddish gray twilight you see the Great River just ahead. You stop to rest beside its waters.

Turn to page 53.

"Yes, bad times are upon us," Arton continues. "But we shall protect ourselves. We have learned to mix powders and call up the fire of the earth in a great blast of noise and heat."

"You mean bombs?"

"We call them *brakpa*. With brakpa and with your help, we shall destroy the Archpods before they destroy us."

"What do you mean, 'with my help'?" you ask.

"You come from the Nether World, where war is the way of life. If you ride with us, our warriors will have courage."

"What are the Kota beasts?"

"You ask too many questions!" the High Raka snaps back. "Now you must answer mine: Will you go with our warriors to attack the Archpods?"

You shrink back from the choice. The High Raka's voice grows stern and cold. "If you are not with us, then you are against us, and we shall deal with you as our enemy."

If you tell the High Raka that you will go with his warriors, turn to page 52.

If you tell him that you won't take part in a war, turn to page 56.

"I'll go with your warriors," you answer.

"Very well," says Arton. "You will stay with Tomo. Vivaldi taught him English, and he will tell you what you need to know."

Immediately one of the Rakas steps forward and takes your arm. "I am Tomo," he says. Then he leads you to the outskirts of the village and into his agon. He brings you woven mats. "You must rest now," he says.

You peer outside at the red-streaked sky. "Doesn't it ever get dark here?"

"We have no night or day," says Tomo. "We measure time by the tides of the Great River. Dr. Vivaldi said two of our tides equal one of your days. It is sleeping tide now."

You realize that you have not slept since you arrived in the Underground Kingdom. How long have you been here? How many tides? Too tired to think about it, you lie down and quickly fall asleep.

Turn to page 54.

Once you've caught your breath, you walk along the river bank and soon reach a crude wooden dock. Two Rakas are guarding their hunting boat, a long flat-bottomed shell fashioned from cluster-leaf wood. Nearby is a smaller boat, one you could paddle yourself. You just might be able to untie it, push off, and get across the river before the guards catch you.

If you try to take the small boat and make a break for the other side, turn to page 57.

If you try to bluff the guards into thinking you have permission to use it, turn to page 58.

When you wake, Tomo gives you a bright pink tanga. You hadn't realized how little you've eaten, and you wolf it down. Smiling, Tomo replaces it with another.

"Someday we will go hunting," says Tomo.

"Are you a hunter?"

"Almost. I must first go on the Hunt of the Black Sun. I must kill a Kota beast."

"A Kota beast? What are they?"

Tomo frowns. "Great toothed animals, with eyes like blue flames and teeth like iron fangs. They live in the darkest, hottest parts of the woods. They tear anything apart, even themselves."

You start to ask about the Hunt of the Black Sun, but Tomo raises a hand. "Now we must talk of war. The Archpods will not expect an attack when the river is low. That is when we shall cross and destroy their boats."

The next morning as the Great River begins to fall, the Rakas load their hunting boat, now called the war boat, with brakpa—crude bombs packed in hollowed logs. You shudder to think that you are about to witness the beginning of a war. But there seems to be no way to avoid it. Before the sleeping tide has ended, Tomo, you, and five hunters set off in the war boat.

Go on to the next page.

The Raka hunters are clumsy at rowing, and the boat is so heavy that a few small waves would easily swamp it. You realize you might be able to swim to shore before the Rakas could turn around and catch you. It's risky, but it's your only chance to avoid the war!

If you dive overboard and swim for shore,
turn to page 61.

If you stick it out in the war boat,
turn to page 62.

"I won't have anything to do with your brakpa," you say. "I am not an enemy of you or of the Archpods."

"Ig krig zaark!" the High Raka says angrily.

Two Raka guards seize you and march you out of the agon. But the moment you get outside, you make a break. You've always been able to run fast when you needed to. In the light gravity, you're even faster. As you dart through the groves of cluster-leaf trees, you can hear the cries of the Rakas from both sides and behind you. But the Great River lies just ahead, and for once you're in luck—there's a crude raft tied up along the shore. You quickly untie it, and push off as you jump aboard. The current soon takes you around a bend in the river and safely out of sight.

You lie low on the raft, afraid of landing until you are well past Rakmara. Now you have time to think. Where will the river take you? What will be your fate?

Turn to page 63.

You quickly reach the boat, but you can't untie the rope! Instantly the Rakas are upon you. Uttering angry cries, they fling their nets over you. One of them blindfolds you. Then they march you along a winding, bumpy path.

"Where are you taking me?" you ask. But the Rakas ignore you, muttering angrily in their own tongue.

Death seems certain. How will they execute you? They seem to like ropes; maybe they will hang you.

As you march on, hour after hour, the air turns colder. You feel your strength ebbing.

Finally the Rakas stop. Exhausted, you crumple to the ground. All is silent, and you fall into a deep sleep.

Turn to page 60.

You think fast. Luckily, you remember the command that the blue-furred Raka gave. You walk up to the guards, smiling. You point in the direction you came from, then to yourself, and then to one of the boats.

"Nar mg calla," you say with authority.

The guards mutter. Then, to your surprise, they smile. One of them unties a boat and motions for you to board it. They must think you're a privileged guest of the High Raka. You quickly get aboard and push off.

As the current takes you around a bend, you notice Archpod settlements on the opposite shore. Soon you spot a good landing place. As you get closer, you notice a band of Archpods standing on the shore. Like the first Rakas you met, they are armed with ropes and nets. They don't look very friendly. You could be in for more trouble than you had with the Rakas.

If you continue in to shore, turn to page 66.

If you start back across the river, turn to page 65.

Hours later you awake, stiff and shaking from the cold. Cautiously you pull off your blindfold. Your captors are gone. All around you is dark brown clay. There are no trees, no water, and no shelter from the cold wind that blows across the vast, empty plain. So this is your intended fate— you will be left to die of exposure under the Black Sun.

It's a long trek across the desert of the Underground Kingdom, but if you can only reach some trees, you may be able to find a warm place to rest. Somehow you know that you'll make it, if you have the will.

Do you?

The End

In a flash you're over the side and swimming for shore. The Rakas yell at you. One of them tries to hit you with an oar while the others stroke furiously, trying to turn their unwilling craft around.

Swimming hard, you hear screams behind you. The war boat has overturned! The brakpa have gone to the bottom, and the Rakas are struggling to save their lives and right the boat. Using all your strength, you swim in to shore and start running for the groves of cluster-leaf trees.

Almost at once you hear a loud, trilling song. Above you is an enormous flying creature with wings stretching twenty feet across! You stare into its great blue-green eyes and at once feel completely safe. You know you've seen it, or at least dreamed of seeing it, before. It's like some kind of angel bird sent to protect you. Without thinking, you leap right onto the creature's back.

Turn to page 22.

Swimming to shore looks too risky. You sit quietly in the boat, hoping for the best. As the war boat nears the middle of the river, the current gets stronger. The Raka warriors can hardly row against it. As the Rakas struggle with their oars, the boat is swept farther and farther downstream.

You wonder where the current will take you, until you hear a sound up ahead that quickly grows into a roar.

"Ig riba!" the Rakas shout. *"Ig zaark!"* They begin to unload the heavy brakpa. Frantically you help, but at the sight of the boiling white rapids ahead, you lose heart. Moments later the boat smashes into the rocks, and you and the Raka warriors are swept away by the raging torrent.

The End

Your raft floats on past marshy banks and yellow clay islands. The river grows narrow as it flows through a deep canyon. Rock cliffs rise up on both sides. You hold on, hoping to reach a place where you can land.

Never have you experienced as dark a night as this. It's as if the river were flowing through a tunnel somewhere in the depths of the earth.

Finally you sleep, and it seems as if a very long time has passed when you awake and find your raft pitching up and down. Why has the river grown so rough? It's still too dark to see much, but at least the stars are out.

Stars? There aren't any stars in the Underground Kingdom. You're not on the river—you're on an ocean!

Go on to page 64.

So, the Great River *must* be an underground link between the earth's seas. The tides were with you and carried you through the earth's mantle and crust to the surface. There's land nearby. And you notice a faint glow on the horizon. Soon the sun will be rising, not the cold Black Sun of the Underground Kingdom, but your own warm, bright, life-giving sun!

The End

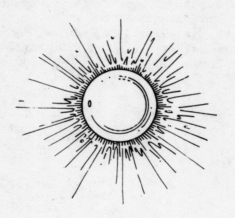

You try to row back to the Rakmara shore, but the current is now so swift that you find yourself being carried downstream. Desperately you try to paddle against it. It's no use. And there's bad trouble up ahead—foaming, white rapids! You hang on for your life, but your raft smashes into a rock with a terrific thunk. One end tilts straight up, dumping you into the wild, swirling waters. You try to grab the raft, but you can't reach it. You start swimming toward shore, but you can't make any headway.

You're not a quitter. You'll go down trying.

The End

Trying to act unafraid, you row straight in to shore, hop out of the boat, and step forward to meet the Archpods. "Hello. I come as a friend!" you call out. But their only response is to take you prisoner and march you back to their village.

You soon find that the Archpods live in agons similar to those of the Rakas. Your captors lead you into the largest one, where you expect to be presented to their chief. Instead, a woman calls your name. It's Dr. Vivaldi!

She hugs you warmly. "I thought I'd never see another human face!" she cries, tears streaming down her cheeks.

One of the guards says something you cannot understand. Then the Archpods march out of the agon, leaving you alone with your friend.

Dr. Vivaldi tells you how she barely survived her fall through the Bottomless Crevasse, how she lived for almost a year with the Rakas and finally swam across the Great River to the land of the Archpods. You tell her of your descent to the Underground Kingdom and your adventures in Rakmara.

"We must set upon a plan," she says. "The Archpods have learned that the Rakas are making bombs. They think we may be Raka spies. That is why you were treated so rudely. They have told me that their chief, the Grand Akpar, will soon decide whether to execute us."

Go on to page 68.

"What can we do?" you ask.

Dr. Vivaldi looks at you thoughtfully, then says, "If there is a war, we cannot expect to survive. I am going to talk to the Grand Akpar. But here, take my gold bracelet. If you give it to the guard, he will let you escape."

"But what will happen to you? I don't want to leave you here. I'll go to the Grand Akpar with you!"

Dr. Vivaldi replies, "Think carefully before you make such a decision."

If you decide to face the Grand Akpar with Dr. Vivaldi, turn to page 70.

If you decide to escape while you still have a chance, turn to page 100.

You're glad that your friends are still alive, and you hurry to meet them. A few minutes later you are exchanging stories of your adventures in the Underground Kingdom. But Larsen and Sneed do not seem happy.

"Is anything wrong?" Dr. Vivaldi finally asks them.

"I'm afraid so," Larsen replies. "We've just inspected the Bottomless Crevasse. The glacier has sealed it tight. We are trapped here forever!"

"We'll never get home now," you say.

"That's the way it looks," says Larsen. "Like it or not, we're pioneers. The only thing for us to do is to make the best of our lives in this new world."

"That's not good enough for me," says Dr. Vivaldi. "We're going to find a way out of here!" She looks at you with a broad smile. "Right?"

"Right," you answer.

The End

"I'll face the Grand Akpar with you."

"That's a brave choice," says Dr. Vivaldi, "but it also would have taken courage to escape." She smiles. "Sometimes there's nothing to do *but* to be brave!" As she speaks three Archpod guards walk into the agon. They motion for you to follow them, but when Dr. Vivaldi tries to join you, they block her way.

"Good luck. . . ." Dr. Vivaldi's voice fades as the guards march you out of the agon.

A few minutes later you are standing in the central agon. Facing you is the Grand Akpar. His long, silky fur is combed like an oval frame around his stern, gray face. A pendant made of smooth black stone hangs from his neck.

He studies you a moment and says, "We have learned from Dr. Vivaldi that you come from the Nether World—the world of warfare. You know much more about such things than we do. You can prove that you are not a Raka spy by telling us how we can defeat them!"

You stand silently, trying to think of what to say.

"I'm waiting," the Grand Akpar says.

What will you do?

If you try to play along with him, turn to page 73.

If you refuse, turn to page 104.

Suddenly, you feel a presence. Looking around, you see pairs of bright blue lights staring at you. Then you see brown bristly faces, iron fangs, and long curled claws. *Kota beasts!* The last sounds you hear are their unearthly shrieks of triumph.

The End

You try to think fast. You don't want to be responsible for killing the Rakas, but you have to sound helpful. "Land your fleet during the sleeping tide," you say. "That way you will surprise them."

"Thank you." The Grand Akpar smiles. "But, if your advice fails, you will be taken to the Mouth of Fire."

The Grand Akpar motions to his guards. They lead you back to Dr. Vivaldi.

You and Dr. Vivaldi wait anxiously, wishing that you could do something to prevent the war. You know that the Archpods are building boats as fast as they can. Dr. Vivaldi pleads with the guards to let her see the Grand Akpar, but they refuse to listen.

One day the Grand Akpar comes to your agon. "Our boats are ready," he says. "We invade Rakmara now."

That sleeping tide, you lie on your bed, dreaming of home. An explosion startles you. The war has begun! The Rakas must have had their bombs ready. You wait anxiously for news of what's happened. Finally it comes—in the form of Archpod guards carrying ropes and nets.

Turn to page 84.

Your head aches. You feel as if you've been run over by a steamroller . . . but a cool hand is pressed against your forehead.

"Don't worry, you're going to be OK," Dr. Vivaldi says. "The radio worked. Help is on the way."

Your face is bruised. It's painful just opening your eyes, but well worth it. For in the bright sunlight you can see ice fields all around you. You're back in Greenland, and right now the whole surface of the earth feels like home!

You look up at Dr. Vivaldi. Her face shows she, too, is in pain. "A broken arm," she explains. "Otherwise, I'm OK."

"We were lucky," you say.

"Yes." She smiles. "The Vertacraft just squeaked through. The crevasse has narrowed two more feet. In another few weeks it will be impossible to get through. You and I will probably be the last ones ever to visit the Underground Kingdom."

"I'm glad we had the chance," you say. "I wouldn't have missed it for the world."

The End

"But what does that have to do with the black hole?" you ask Bruckner.

The professor pauses to fill his pipe. "As I explained in my published theory, a tiny black hole lodged in the center of the earth more than a billion years ago. It pulled the interior of the earth—everything except for the crust and mantle—into itself, leaving the earth hollowed out like a Halloween pumpkin. That is what the gravity readings tell us."

"Then where is the Underground Kingdom?"

"It is the whole interior surface of the earth. And if you stood there and looked straight up, you would see the black hole. It would look exactly like our sun except that it would be jet black."

Professor Bruckner lights his pipe, then says, "I did not expect to undertake this mission for some months. I only planned to inspect the crevasse and test the Vertacraft, but the crevasse is closing rapidly. I must make the descent today. Otherwise, my return path might be blocked. Who will volunteer to come with me?"

Turn to page 77.

76

When you tell Dr. Vivaldi of the advice you gave the Grand Akpar, she shakes your hand. "I would have said the same thing. If our destiny is to die at the hands of the Archpods, it will not be your fault."

Now three tides have passed. You and Dr. Vivaldi are still waiting for the news that will seal your fate.

It must be midway through the second sleeping tide when the guards awaken you. A moment later, the Grand Akpar walks into your agon. With him is the High Raka.

"The Archpods and the Rakas have made peace," says Akpar. "From now on we shall build boats for both tribes, and there shall be no bombs!"

Turn to page 78..

One after another, the team members shake their heads.

Finally Bruckner turns to you. "Well?"

You hesitate. You don't want to risk your life. But this could be the only chance of finding your lost friends.

If you decide to go with him, turn to page 35.

If you decide not to risk it, turn to page 33.

From then on you and Dr. Vivaldi are treated like honored guests. The Archpods bring you baskets heaped with tanga, and cakes made from golden grain. They show you their mineral pools where you swim in the swirling, bubbly water. Later you lie in the warmth of the glowing rocks, then cool off under the Black Sun.

A few tides later the Grand Akpar pays you a visit. "Would you like to stay longer and explore the Underground Kingdom?" he asks. "We shall lend you three hunters to guide you. Or, if you wish, you may return to the Nether World."

"Which do you prefer?" Dr. Vivaldi asks you. "There may still be a chance to return home, though the risks are great."

If you say that you want to explore the Underground Kingdom, turn to page 81.

If you say that you want to try to return to the surface, turn to page 82.

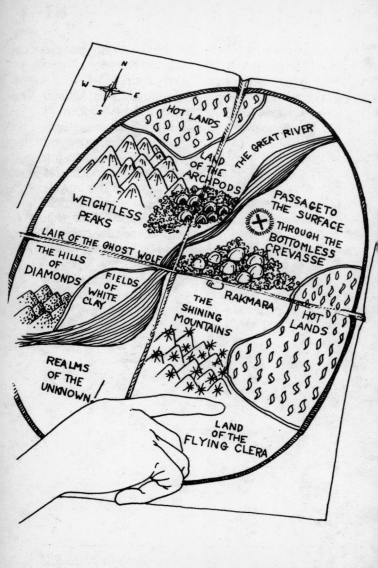

"This may be the only chance earth people have to explore the Underground Kingdom," you say, "and I don't want to pass it up."

"I'm glad to hear you say that." Dr. Vivaldi unfolds a map of the Underground Kingdom. "I made this map from what the Rakas and Archpods have told me. Although the Underground Kingdom has an area sixty percent as large as the surface of the earth, only a very small portion is cool enough to be habitable. Most of the land is too hot to set foot on. It is the molten red rock, you know, that provides the reddish glow that lights this dim world. If it were not for the tremendous cooling effect of the Black Sun, life could not exist here."

Sometimes Dr. Vivaldi gets too scientific for you. "Where do you think we should explore?" you ask.

Turn to page 83.

"If there's a chance of making it," you say, "I'd like to try to get home."

"Then we must hurry," says Dr. Vivaldi. "Akpar, there is not much you can do but lead us to the crater where we arrived."

The Grand Akpar speaks in his own tongue to a guard, who quickly leaves the chamber. Turning to you he says, "I shall have a boat readied to take you across the Great River. Come then, we will guide you back to the secret canyon."

After a three-tides' journey you and Dr. Vivaldi, guided by a party of Archpods, reach the Bottomless Crevasse. Dr. Vivaldi runs toward a small metal craft on the crater floor.

"A Vertacraft!" she says. "With luck this will get us back to the earth's surface."

Dr. Vivaldi gives instructions to the Archpods, who then use their ropes to suspend the craft directly over the shaft of the crevasse. You and Dr. Vivaldi thank your hosts and bid them farewell. The canopy cover closes. You watch anxiously as Dr. Vivaldi checks out the instruments. "Are you ready?" she asks.

"Ready." You grit your teeth as the Vertacraft accelerates into the crevasse and begins the 800-mile descent to the surface of the earth. You're pressed flat against your seat. The g force is terrific! It's getting worse. What's happening? Can't Dr. Vivaldi stop it? You're blacking out.

Turn to page 74.

"There are three areas that fascinate me equally," she answers, "so I'll let you choose among them. To the west are the Weightless Peaks, where you become lighter and lighter, the higher you climb. To the south are the Hills of Diamonds. The Archpods are afraid to go there. They say it is too close to what they call the Lair of the Ghost Wolf."

"What lies across the Great River?" you ask. "Beyond Rakmara."

"The Shining Mountains. There we may find creatures whom the Archpods call the Flying Clera. They are great birds, who may be the true rulers of the Underground Kingdom—higher even than humans on the evolutionary scale. What would you prefer?"

If you decide to explore the Weightless Peaks,
turn to page 85.

If you decide to go to the Hills of Diamonds,
turn to page 88.

If you decide to explore the Shining Mountains,
turn to page 36.

"You betrayed us," says the head guard. "The Rakas threw bombs into our boats. Nearly all of them were lost. Many of our hunters were killed." He turns to the others behind him. "Bind them and take them to the Mouth of Fire."

You cry out for mercy, but you know there will be none.

The End

A few tides later you and Dr. Vivaldi set out for the Weightless Peaks. With you is a young Archpod named Katu, chosen because she speaks your language.

On the trek from the Archpod village to the Weightless Peaks, Katu tells you the legend of the Archpods who traveled through a shaft that led to a new universe. Few Archpods believed there could be such a place. Most of them thought that the earth was infinitely thick, that nothing could lie beyond it. "Now that human beings have arrived, we know that there is a whole new world right under our feet. We call your world the Nether World," she says. "We are curious about it. But we are also afraid of it, and of its creatures who could destroy us."

"Sometimes we human beings are afraid of ourselves," you reply.

After hiking for fourteen tides, you begin to climb—first gentle hills, then steep mountains. You tire under the weight of your pack, but Dr. Vivaldi urges you on. "It will soon be easier," she says. And she is proven correct, for as you struggle up the next steep hill, you feel your pack growing lighter, and you feel lighter too. Ahead of you, Katu is bounding up the higher peaks like a mountain gazelle.

Turn to page 87.

"Now you can see," says Dr. Vivaldi, "how on the Weightless Peaks the higher you go, the lighter you'll get. Look!" She points to the highest peak of all. Its top is a spire jutting into the sky. A thin plume of smoke rises from the top.

"It must be a volcano," you say.

"No," says Dr. Vivaldi. "Something else is going on. The mountain's gravity at its peak is so weak that dust is being pulled off by the tremendous gravity of the Black Sun."

"I bet I only weigh five or six pounds," you say. "I could easily climb to the top of that spire."

"Better not," says Dr. Vivaldi.

You realize that if you're so light, the huge boulders around you can't weigh very much either. You decide to test your theory. You nudge a boulder twice your size. It rolls into another boulder. Then above you, Katu screams, "Avalanche!"

Turn to page 106.

Certainly the Hills of Diamonds must be an amazing sight. And, if you ever do make it back to the surface, it wouldn't hurt to have a few dozen diamonds in your pockets—you could be rich for life!

The Archpods provide you and Dr. Vivaldi with their largest boat for the trip down the Great River to the diamond hills.

After a journey of six tides, you hear a roaring up ahead. The Archpods quickly beach the boat. "We can go no farther," the leader tells you. "There are deep canyons and fierce rapids ahead. We must go on foot across the field of white clay."

You soon find that the white clay is extremely hot. Your feet would burn up were it not for the light gravity of the underworld that permits you to race across the field in great leaps.

Finally you reach cooler ground. Ahead of you is a dazzling vision: dozens of little hills of brilliant diamonds!

Turn to page 91.

You push the Emergency-Reverse button. Instantly you are pressed to your seat, almost crushed by the forces as the retro-rockets fire. The artificial weight squeezes the air out of your lungs. Then, slowly, the pressure eases. For a moment you're completely weightless. Your heart is pounding as you check the depth meter. The Vertacraft is rising!

"*You fool. What have you done?*" Bruckner sounds wilder than ever.

"I'm returning us to the surface, Professor." Your voice is cool. You feel confident now that the Vertacraft has responded to your command.

"Why didn't you ask?" Bruckner's voice is bitter. "The auto-return isn't programmed to adjust for this gravitation."

Bruckner sounds more sane now. It's you who's beginning to feel crazy. "What will happen then?" you ask.

Suddenly the darkness is replaced by blinding sunlight. The Vertacraft has reached the surface, yet it's still accelerating, shooting up into the stratosphere!

"Can't we bring it back down?"

"I'm afraid not, my foolish young friend," Bruckner replies in a cold, dead tone. "It's a command procedure. There's no override. We're headed into outer space. Within a few hours we'll be frozen solid."

The End

"Look at all those diamonds," you say. "I'm surprised the Archpods haven't already taken them."

"Villa tarem, zaark!" One of the Archpods is screaming. Several of them point to the north. *"Tarem Agax!"*

You can't see anything unusual, but the Archpods are deserting you, racing back across the field.

"What's going on? Do you see anything?" you ask Dr. Vivaldi.

She shakes her head, seemingly as confused as you are. "It must be the ghost wolf. What we are witnessing may be more interesting than the diamond hills themselves. We may be in the presence of a life force that the Archpods can see but we can't. Or maybe what they see is an illusion, and *we* are right in thinking nothing is there. This is something that has always interested me: different realities for different observers."

"I don't think we have time to figure it out now," you say.

"You may be right," Dr. Vivaldi admits. "In any event, I would guess that the Archpods have good reasons for their fears. Are you willing to risk continuing on to the Hills of Diamonds, or do you want to turn back?"

*If you say you want to continue,
turn to page 94.*

*If you say you want to turn back,
turn to page 97.*

"I think I know why the Archpods and Rakas avoid this beautiful land," says Dr. Vivaldi. "They are conditioned to the dim red light of the Great River valley. The broad daylight here bothers Mopur as much as it would bother us to live in semidarkness."

"Why *is* it so bright—?"

You are interrupted by cries from Mopur. *"Clera! The Flying Clera!"*

Craning your neck, you see several great bird-like creatures swooping across the sky.

"They are like nothing that has ever lived on the surface," says Dr. Vivaldi. "They may have evolved on some other planet."

You fall silent as the music of the Flying Clera begins—a great chorus you hear not only with your ears, but with your whole body.

Like you, Dr. Vivaldi seems hypnotized. "They sound truly angelic," she says.

But Mopur tugs at your sleeves. "This is not the place for us," he says. "We are not ready."

"I have a strong feeling that we must turn back," says Dr. Vivaldi.

"Yes," you say, "I have the same feeling. Some force is pulling us back."

Dr. Vivaldi's gaze is fixed on the Shining Mountains. "The Flying Clera are a very advanced species," she explains. "They have the ability to project their feelings onto us. Their presence and purpose here is a mystery that I suspect we are not yet ready to understand, but I feel certain that they represent a force of good in the universe."

"If the Flying Clera are so advanced," you say,

"why don't they rule the Underground Kingdom?"

Dr. Vivaldi smiles. "I don't know, but I would guess that not wanting to rule others is part of being advanced."

At that moment you are overcome by a strong desire to return home, to the surface of the earth. You exchange glances with Dr. Vivaldi. "Do you have the same feeling I do?" you ask.

She nods and motions you to follow.

Turn to page 98.

"Let's get to those diamonds," you cry. And you run toward the points of sparkling white light.

At the same time you begin choking on thick sulphurous fumes. Behind you, thunder rumbles from the ground!

Dr. Vivaldi has reached the first hill of diamonds. "They're the real thing!" she calls, sifting them through her hands. "Within a few yards of us are more diamonds than are worn by all the people on earth!"

"Look!" you shout, for now the fields of white clay are bubbling like boiling soup. Pale yellow gases rise from cracks in the ground.

"We are trapped." Dr. Vivaldi's voice sounds far away. "By the time the claybeds stop erupting, these fumes will . . . put . . . us . . . to . . . sleep." She coughs and staggers a few feet up a small hill of diamonds. "Quick, over here!" she calls.

Gasping, you stumble up the hill and collapse in a mound of diamonds. Dr. Vivaldi breathes deeply. "We're safe for the moment. This hill is well above the toxic gases." Her voice is drowned out by the ground thunder.

Go on to the next page.

"It looks like we're stuck here with all these millions of diamonds," you say.

"Maybe not," replies Dr. Vivaldi. "The eruptions are quite localized. The gases are rising, but I think we can make it across the deadly strip of clay—it's less than a hundred feet, I'd guess. There's only one way to do it—take a deep breath and run as fast as you can. Don't breathe until you absolutely have to. Are you willing to try?"

If you're willing to run for it, turn to page 101.

If not, turn to page 102.

"I don't believe the Archpods are running from nothing," you say. "Let's get out of here!"

"OK!" Dr. Vivaldi starts back across the field of white clay, and you are right behind her.

Running as fast as you can, still loaded down by your pack, you feel a rumbling beneath your feet. The ground begins to split apart. Great slivers of clay are heaved up. Wide cracks open around you. You think back to when you fell into the Bottomless Crevasse in Greenland. This time there may be no escape.

You see Dr. Vivaldi crawling on her hands and knees, trying to work her way from the edge of a crevice. The ground is shaking so hard you can no longer stand. The air is filled with yellowish haze as sulphurous fumes escape from beneath the surface. Looking up, you see the blurred gray form of a wolf looming as large as a mountain, crowding out half the sky! Its bared, curving teeth are like rows of elephant tusks. Its hot breath takes your breath away, and the red world around you goes black.

Turn to page 103.

"We mustn't waste time," says Dr. Vivaldi. "The Bottomless Crevasse closes a bit more every day."

Led by the Archpod guide, you begin the long trek back to the Great River.

Six tides have passed before your party descends the mountain trail into the valley of the Great River. You are eager to get back to the Bottomless Crevasse—your only hope of returning to the surface of the earth and home. As you strain your eyes, looking for the Raka village, you see two figures headed toward you up the trail. They're human!

"Can it be?" you cry.

Dr. Vivaldi stares through her mini-binoculars. "No doubt about it," she says, "Larsen and Sneed! They made it here alive!"

Turn to page 69.

At the change of tide, Dr. Vivaldi leaves for her interview with the Grand Akpar. Only one Raka is left to guard you. You hand him the gold bracelet. Taking it, he smiles broadly. You hurry past him, but another guard is standing outside the agon. You wheel past him and run for it. The surprised Archpod yells; you soon hear others chasing you. But in a few moments you reach the shelter of the cluster-leaf groves, and as you go deeper into the woods, you are relieved that you no longer hear the Archpods behind you. It's strange, though, that they didn't follow you into the woods.

Turn to page 72.

"Let's run for it!" you shout.

Dr. Vivaldi scans the bubbling fields of clay. "I think I know the best direction to run, so I'll go first, and you follow." You can just barely hear her voice. *"Remember to hold your breath, and don't forget to . . . "* Her voice is cut off by more thunder as she races across the white clay.

What was she trying to tell you not to forget?

No more time to think! You take a deep breath and *run!*

Turn to page 108.

"I'm worried we won't make it," you say. "Maybe the eruptions will end soon, if we just wait here awhile."

"Maybe so," Dr. Vivaldi observes without looking at you. "And maybe it will get worse."

The two of you sit, waiting. Soon a breeze begins to blow. A minute later you are coughing and sputtering as the toxic gases rise over your hill. You try not to breathe more than you can help, but your vision blurs and your head spins. You can't even sit up. . . .

It's strange. Diamonds are the hardest substance in the world; yet, if they are several feet deep and you lie down on them, they make a soft bed. And so the end comes easily for you.

The End

You are lying on a hammock woven of fine *clima* vines. You feel flushed and feverish, yet happy: you're alive! Dr. Vivaldi is beside you. She brushes a cool, wet cloth across your forehead.

"Where are we?" you ask. "How did we get out of there? Did you see the ghost wolf?"

"We're back with the Archpods," Dr. Vivaldi says, smiling. "And I did see a great beast with tongues of fire, but in truth there was no wolf, nor any other beast. And the cracks in the field were only a few inches wide, just wide enough to release a poisonous gas from beneath the ground. A few whiffs of it was enough to make us hallucinate and have the most horrible nightmares. It's fascinating that the gas causes such a specific common vision—I'd like to research this some more. In any event, we were lucky to be close to the edge when I realized what was happening. I was able to pull you away so you could get fresh air."

"Thanks," you say. "After this I'm not going to be afraid of anything in the Underground Kingdom."

"That's good," she replies, "because we still have a whole new world to explore!"

The End

"I won't help you fight the Rakas," you tell the Grand Akpar. "War is a terrible thing. Your villages will be destroyed and your people will be killed. Our wars have *always* brought grief."

The Grand Akpar is silent for a time. "Then it would be like that here," he finally says. "But how can we avoid war? If we do nothing, the Rakas will destroy us."

"Talk to them," you say. "Work out a plan for peace."

"No," he says, shaking his head. "We can't trust them."

"And they think they can't trust you! You must tell them what you fear from them, and ask what they fear from you. You might discover that you fear the same things. Once you've reached an understanding, you can work out a plan that will let the Rakas and the Archpods live in peace.

Go on to the next page.

The Grand Akpar paces from one side of the agon to the other. Finally he stops and stares into your eyes. You shrink back from his stern gaze. "I will try what you suggest," he says. "Meanwhile you will be kept under guard with Dr. Vivaldi. If all goes well, you shall be freed, and we will do everything we can to make you happy here. When you are ready to return to the Nether World, we shall help you."

You start to thank the Grand Akpar, but he holds up his hand. "Do not thank me until I tell you this: If we are betrayed and the Rakas attack, you and Dr. Vivaldi will die."

There is not much you can say, and you would hardly have time anyway, for the guards quickly lead you away.

Turn to page 76.

It's an avalanche all right, but the boulders are rolling *up* the mountain! Panicked, you run toward Katu. The boulders are coming right at you. At near zero gravity they're being pulled toward the Black Sun.

"You've got to run *down*!" Dr. Vivaldi shouts.

But the boulders have cut off your escape. The only thing you can do is run up the mountain, trying to keep out of their path. You're running higher and faster, leaping fifty feet at a time. Ahead of you, Katu flies off the mountain. Before you can stop yourself your feet lose touch with the ground, and you're in the air, being swept higher and higher, straight toward the Black Sun!

You've read that a black hole might somehow be an entrance to another universe. If only that were possible! It's your only chance once you reach the Black Sun. A chance in a million maybe, but still a chance . . .

The End

You made it!

Across the fields of white clay and safely back to the land of the Archpods.

And, if you remembered to fill your pockets with diamonds before you ran across the field of white clay, you're *very* rich!

The End

ABOUT THE AUTHOR

EDWARD PACKARD, a graduate of Princeton University and Columbia Law School, practiced law in New York and Connecticut before turning to writing full time. He developed the unique storytelling approach used in the Choose Your Own Adventure® series while thinking up stories for his children, Caroline, Andrea, and Wells.

ABOUT THE ILLUSTRATOR

ANTHONY KRAMER graduated from the Paier School of Art in Hamden, Connecticut, where he received the Children's Book Illustration award. He has been an editorial cartoonist, an architectural artist, and a designer of children's toy packages. He has illustrated eight books for children, including *Secret of the Pyramids* by Richard Brightfield for Bantam's Choose Your Own Adventure® series. Mr. Kramer lives in New York City where he loves to walk, run, and bicycle.

CHOOSE YOUR OWN ADVENTURE

☐	25763	PRISONER OF THE ANT PEOPLE #25	$2.25
☐	25916	THE PHANTOM SUBMARINE #26	$2.25
☐	23867	THE HORROR OF HIGH RIDGE #27	$1.95
☐	23868	MOUNTAIN SURVIVAL #28	$1.95
☐	23865	TROUBLE ON PLANET EARTH #29	$1.95
☐	23937	THE CURSE OF BATTLESLEA HALL #30	$1.95
☐	24099	VAMPIRE EXPRESS #31	$1.95
☐	25764	TREASURE DIVER #32	$2.25
☐	25918	THE DRAGON'S DEN #33	$2.25
☐	24344	THE MYSTERY OF HIGHLAND CREST #34	$1.95
☐	25967	JOURNEY TO STONEHENGE #35	$2.25
☐	24522	THE SECRET TREASURE OF TIBET #36	$1.95
☐	25778	WAR WITH THE EVIL POWER MASTER #37	$2.25
☐	25818	SUPERCOMPUTER #39	$1.95
☐	24679	THE THRONE OF ZEUS #40	$1.95
☐	26062	SEARCH FOR MOUNTAIN GORILLAS #41	$2.25
☐	24720	THE MYSTERY OF ECHO LODGE #42	$1.95
☐	24822	GRAND CANYON ODYSSEY #43	$1.95
☐	24892	THE MYSTERY OF URA SENKE #44	$1.95
☐	24963	YOU ARE A SHARK #45	$1.95
☐	24991	THE DEADLY SHADOW #46	$1.95
☐	25069	OUTLAWS OF SHERWOOD FOREST #47	$1.95
☐	25134	SPY FOR GEORGE WASHINGTON #48	$1.95
☐	25177	DANGER AT ANCHOR MINE #49	$2.25
☐	25296	RETURN TO CAVE OF TIME #50	$2.25

Prices and availability subject to change without notice.

BLAST INTO THE PAST!

TIME MACHINE

Each of these books is a time machine and you are at the controls . . .

☐	23601	**SECRETS OF THE KNIGHTS #1** J. Gasperini	$1.95
☐	25399	**SEARCH FOR DINOSAURS #2** D. Bischoff	$2.25
☐	25619	**SWORD OF THE SAMURAI #3** M. Reaves & S. Perry	$2.25
☐	25616	**SAIL WITH PIRATES #4** J. Gasperini	$2.25
☐	25606	**CIVIL WAR SECRET AGENT #5** Steve Perry	$2.25
☐	25797	**THE RINGS OF SATURN #6** Arthur Cover	$2.25
☐	24722	**ICE AGE EXPLORER #7** Dougal Dixon	$1.95
☐	25073	**THE MYSTERY OF ATLANTIS #8** Jim Gasperini	$2.25
☐	25180	**WILD WEST RIDER #9** Stephen Overholser	$2.25
☐	25300	**AMERICAN REVOLUTIONARY #10** Arthur Byron	$2.25
☐	25431	**MISSION TO WORLD WAR II #11** S. Nanus & M. Kornblatt	$2.25
☐	25538	**SEARCH FOR THE NILE #12** Robert W. Walker	$2.25

Prices and availability subject to change without notice.

Shop at home
for quality childrens books
and save money, too.

Now you can order books for the whole family from Bantam's latest listing of hundreds of titles including many fine children's books. *And* this special offer gives you an opportunity to purchase a Bantam book for only 50¢. Here's how:

By ordering any five books at the regular price per order, you can also choose any other single book listed (up to $4.95 value) for just 50¢. Some restrictions do apply, so for further details send for Bantam's listing of titles today.